Edward Melcher

A Sketch of the Destruction of the Willey Family

by the White Mountain slide on the night of August 28, 1826

Edward Melcher

A Sketch of the Destruction of the Willey Family
by the White Mountain slide on the night of August 28, 1826

ISBN/EAN: 9783337288419

Printed in Europe, USA, Canada, Australia, Japan

Cover: Foto ©Andreas Hilbeck / pixelio.de

More available books at **www.hansebooks.com**

A SKETCH

OF THE

DESTRUCTION

—— OF THE ——

WILLEY FAMILY

——BY THE——

WHITE MOUNTAIN SLIDE,

On the Night of August 28, 1826,

RELATED

BY EDWARD MELCHER,

The only survivor of the party who discovered and removed
the bodies of the unfortunate family from the
ruins, on the 31st day of August, 1826.

LANCASTER, N. H.:
J. S. PEAVEY, BOOK AND JOB PRINTER.
1880.

A SKETCH

OF THE

DESTRUCTION

—— OF THE ——

WILLEY FAMILY

——BY THE——

WHITE MOUNTAIN SLIDE,

ON THE NIGHT OF AUGUST 28, 1826,

RELATED

BY EDWARD MELCHER,

The only survivor of the party who discovered and removed
the bodies of the unfortunate family from the
ruins, on the 31st day of August, 1826.

LANCASTER, N. H.:
J. S. PEAVEY, BOOK AND JOB PRINTER.
1880.

than perpendicular, the top projecting over that portion that rested on the ground—so much so as to form caves.

It had got to be well toward noon and in all this time we had seen nothing to indicate where the bodies of the unfortunate family could be found. Seeing large numbers of flies about the entrance, I was led to search one of the caves above mentioned. I crawled in quite a number of feet, and discovered a man's hand jammed in between two logs. I came out and indicated to Thomas Hart and Stephen Willey where to dig. We soon came to the body of the man whose hand I had seen. It proved to be that of David Allen, a hired man of the Willeys. Directly behind the body of Allen was that of Mrs. Willey. Both were entirely denuded and terribly mangled, especially about their heads. The back part of Mrs. Willey's head was entirely jammed off. Large numbers of people were soon on the spot—but three of us did all the digging. As fast as we got the bodies out of the jam they were enshrouded in sheets, and buried where the new Hotel now stands, in which place they remained until the following December, when their bodies found a final resting place on the Willey farm in North Conway. Mr. Willey was found below the jam, —drowned in the brook, or possibly killed by the timbers of the demolished barn, under

ker liberated the animals in the stables and went down to Judge Hall's that night, where we met him. Twelve of us, Ebenezar Tasker, Jonathan and Joshua Rodgers, Samuel Tuttle, Abram Allen, Samuel Stillings, Isaac Fall, Levi Parker, Mr. Eastman, Abel Crawford and myself started that night for the Notch.

When we got to the Sawyer river it was so deep the old gentleman Crawford was afraid to attempt to ford it, and I took him on my back and carried him over.

We arrived at Crawford's at eleven o'clock p. m., where we had supper We then went up through the Notch, six miles; the bridges were all gone—and the roads, too, some of the way. We struggled forward till long past midnight, frequently wading through slough-holes, when we arrived at the Willey House.

As soon as it was light in the morning we commenced the search. As the family had not been heard from, we were satisfied they had been buried under the mountain slide, the course of which, presented an appalling spectacle. The track of the slide reached to within three feet of the house, and had carried away one corner of the barn. Across the course of the slide, the rocks, gravel and trees were piled and mixed in awful confusion for a great distance. It seemed to have suddenly stopped, for the advanced part of the avalanche was more

structing the river, raising the water over the path we had just trod, to more than ten feet deep and overflowing the little meadow to the extent of fifteen acres with gravel, rocks and uprooted trees from the mountains. This shower or torrent, lasted four hours and then cleared off bright star-light, the rumbling of the slides continuing most terrific for half an hour.

We stopped at our neighbor's till morning, when I went back to find my little farm entirely ruined, my barn-frame and all the materials for finishing it, swept away, my cow and seven or eight pigs saved only by taking refuge on a manure heap, the hens perched on the ridge of the house, the river running through the cellar.

I loitered about pretty much all day, for I could not cross the river—(it was a river then) —and could not make up my mind what to do. The next day some of my neighbors came, and we built a boat and got across the river, taking with us old Abel Crawford, who came later. We then went to Judge Hall's tavern in Bartlett. There we met a man telling the Judge the story of the *great slide* at the Willey House, he not knowing at that time the full extent of the disaster.

This man, whose name was Barker, stopped the previous night alone at the Willey House (for it was a tavern)—thinking the family were safe at their neighbor's, Abel Crawford's. Bar-

IN the year 1821 I commenced upon a farm in the town of Bartlett, Carroll County, N. H. I bought 100 acres of wild land, and only with good courage and a strong arm, had, in 1826, partially cleared up my small farm from the primitive forest. I had got most of the material together for building me a nice barn, the frame of which was already up. August 28, of the year above mentioned, it commenced to rain in the morning, and rained nearly all day, by showers, till night-fall—then the big shower commenced. I began to have some fears by that time that we were not quite safe, as our house was near a brook that ran through a little meadow, and this rook had already grown to be a good sized 'ver. Accordingly I took my wife and four children and started for a neighbor's who lived pout three-fourths of a mile away on the up- ands. The bridge on which we crossed the brook in front of our house was partially afloat. Not more than a minute after we were well over, we heard the roar of the rumbling waters rushing from the mountain-side near by—sounding like heavy thunder. Down came the slide ob-

which he was found. The youngest boy was found a little in rear of his mother, and the oldest girl below her father, in the brook. A young man about twenty years old, named David Nickerson, whom the Willeys had brought up, was also among the lost, his body being found the next day about a foot deeper in the rubbish, and some four feet from the others. The bodies of the three remaining children of the Willey's were never found.

The following are the names of the lost :

Samuel Willey, Jr.,	aged 38	years.
Polly L. Willey,	" 35	"
Eliza Ann Willey,	" 13	"
Jeremiah L. Willey,	" 11	"
Martha G. Willey,	" 9	"
Sally Willey,	" 5	"
Elbridge G. Willey,	" 7	"
David Nickerson,	" 21	"
David Allen,	" 37	"

The first three and last three were found, but the other three are where the avalanche over took them that fatal hour.

It may be asked why the family left their house, since the house was not injured. On the 25th of June, preceding, there had been a slide not far from the Willey House. It had been raining all day, and at five o'clock p. m., the slide commenced and the trees stood straight until the slide had gone some eight rods before they fell over ; this slide came down within two or three rods of the barn. Nicholas Tuttle, now of Jefferson, was an eye witness of this slide, having gone to Willey's that day to repair boots for the men at work for Willey upon the road through the Notch. This slide filled the road for forty or fifty rods ; this had so alarmed the family that they built a camp (as it was called,) farther down the intervale, in which they intended to take refuge in case the mountain should again threaten them, and it is supposed the family were overwhelmed in their attempt to reach this shelter. As the Willey House stood directly in the line of the avalanche, it would have been swept away but for a rock near the corner of the house, well sunken in the ground, which proved to be a barrier that turned the current by first arresting a large spruce tree and then what was immediately behind, till the mass was piled up as high as the house, and so near I could easily step from the rubbish to the top of the building. Thus the house was saved and the camp they failed to reach was swept away.

These terrific scenes which I have attempted to narrate made a deep impression on my memory, and to-day, at 83 years of age, they seem as vivid as on the fated day of their occurrence.

The foregoing hastily written sketch, so gladly received by the thousands of visitors to the scene of the terrible disaster, has led others to undertake a description of the Willey Slide, and their sketches, printed in the public journals, being based principally upon accounts given by persons not present, but only related from hearsay testimony, contains many errors. That those error may be corrected, and a true account given, by the only surviving member of the little party of twelve who, on the night of Aug. 30, arrived upon the spot, to view the work of the terrible storm, has induced me to give some further incidents connected with the sad disaster. The narrator in the sketch of C. L. Morrison, being then only seventeen years old, was not present and did not visit the scene ;— and her account, though correct in many particulars, contains many errors. J. H. Hall, who afterwards became the husband of the narrator, was three years younger than his wife, being born in August, 1812, and, at the time of the slide, was fourteen years of age. He did not accompany the searching party, and was not present at the time the bodies were recovered. It appears that her information was obtained from this lad, and it could not be expected to be as correct as from an eye witness.

On the third page I give the names of the twelve who composed the searching party.

Neither Lieut. Stanton or his dog were present. I have already stated that I first discovered the situation of the bodies—the gathering of flies led to the discovery, but no dog was present to show his superior wisdom. It may be rough on the dog to spoil this beautiful story, yet it is of more importance that history should record facts as they actually existed, and not as fancy would paint them.

Mr. Allen's right hand was extended toward Mrs. Willey and about two feet from her left hand, and it appeared as though they had joined hands in his attempt to save her, but when found were not joined. Both were lying upon their faces. Mr. Allen's left hand was fast between two logs—it being dark in the place, nothing could be seen, but by reaching in to discover if I could, what attracted the flies, I took hold of a hand and examined each finger and thumb to satisfy myself that it was a man's hand, and it proved to be Mr. Allen's.

Mr. Allen and Mrs. Willey being the first bodies recovered were nude. While we were digging out these bodies, others discovered Mr. Willey's body down the brook four or five rods from where we were digging—he was clothed with the exception of one coat sleeve, which was torn entirely off. Mr. Willey was fast under a timber torn from the barn. I had crossed the brook several times on the timber, but did not

iscover Mr. Willey, and he was not found un-
il tʰ ; water had lowered in the brook, and one
neè was seen above the water.   These three
;ere found on Thursday, the first day of our
earch, and not Friday as Mrs. Hall states.

My three boys, William aged 8 years, Ed-
;ard aged 6 years, and Lee aged 3 years, were
ttending school on the opposite side of the
;aco river, about one and one-half miles from
ome, at the time of the alide.   On their way
ome they had to cross what was called the
;tanton Bridge, made of round logs, about one-
alf mile from Raser brook, over which the
ettler's road passed ; when the children arriv-
d, the water was over the bridge.   The oldest
oy was afraid to cross, but the second boy ran
cross the bridge, and immediately returned
nd taking the youngest in his arms immedi-
tely re-crossed, and William followed.   Just as
1ey were all safe over, the bridge went off in
1e flood.   Had they delayed for one moment
1ey must all have been lost, as the bridge was
wept away and there would have been no re-
'eat.   They arrived home about sunset.

I have endeavored to give a true account of this terrible disaster, and in closing my little book I give the following account of the flood as given by Mrs. Coffin now living in Lancaster :

On the 28th of August, 1826, (I think,) it rained very gently most of the day, with no sign of any rise of the waters around us. My father's name was Ebenezer Stillings I then had a step-mother, and the family consisted of seven persons—my father, step-mother, four children, and a Mrs. Grey, wife of a son of my step-mother. My brothers' names were Leander and Ira ; my sister's name was Cordelia.

We lived in what was then called Hart's Location, between Sawyer River and Stoney Brook. In front ran the Saco river ; back of us was a small brook which was never dry. In time of high water the Saco river overflowed, running into the brook on one side of the house and returning to the Saco on the other side, leaving the house on an island.

At this time my father had a yoke of oxen, two cows and some young stock. This stock was on the upland beyond the brook, and so were safe. He had also, a good flock of sheep, four swine and a flock of geese, all of which were near the house on the island.

At sundown there seemed only a possibility of the water rising. We had a number of yards of cloth on the ground bleaching ; Mrs. Grey and I went out to move it on to higher ground, farther from the brook. After spreading it in the orchard we left the large empty tub close by.

After dark the storm increased and about nine o'clock the sheep came around the house for shelter. I went out to hold the lantern inside the barn while father went to drive the sheep in. The rain was now falling in torrents and poured from the roof in such a sheet that he could not see the light, although I stood as near as possible.   *   *   *

Mrs. Grey was anxious about the cloth, and father and I went out to bring it in. We found the wash-tub two-thirds full of water that it had caught during the storm. On returning to the house we found the water was rushing into the cellar, and in a moment it rose above the floor. We went up stairs, and father followed us after he had put fire into the oven to save it. In a few minutes the house began to rock like a cradle—so that we were obliged to hold the candle. This commotion lasted about two and one-half hours, when it suddenly ceased. We could do nothing but wait and wonder. This must have been about half-past eleven. At about one o'clock in the morning the rain ceased, and soon the water began to lower in

the house.   After day-light, when the water had
settled out of the house, we went down stairs
and found the mud had washed in at least
six inches deep, with indications that the water
had been up to the windows.

It was sunrise before we could get out of
the house, and father, after looking around,
came in to tell us what he thought had saved
our lives.   The small stones had been washed
away from the underpinning and under one
corner was a large rock, about six inches below
the corner-post, a small birch tree that had been
washed out above, was found so wedged under
the sill as to suddenly stop the rocking.   One
of the shotes was found braced against a stump,
half covered with water, but alive ; two were
lost and never found. The sheep were all safe
but had been nearly submerged in water.   The
geese were found about two miles below. Under
one end of the barn the earth was washed away
so that at about eleven o'clock A. M. the building fell and most of the hay was lost. We lost
our crops of potatoes, corn and beans, but the
wheat and oats were in the barn and were
removed and saved.

Nicholas Tuttle, my sister's husband, was
the first to arrive. He felled a tree across Sawyer river and crossed on that.   The next person
who came was a man who had spent Tuesday
night (the night following the rain) at the Wil-

ley House. He came Wednesday, and said he could find none of the family, and thought they must all be dead.

The following extracts from Mrs. Ethan A. Crawford's book, published many years ago, entitled "Guide and Historical Relics of the White Mountains," will be found full of interest. That book having long been out of print, I take the liberty of presenting some of the important facts given in that most excellent work :

The name of E. A. Crawford is deeply chiseled upon the rocks of this gigantic Mount built by nature (Mt. Washington) ; and the lady who shared in life his joys and sorrows has, in her White Mountain History, reared a testimonial to his memory. Will not my humble tribute of a stone, laid in silence upon his grave, be accepted by all who pleasantly cherish the remembrance of "Ethan of the Hills," or the "White Mountain Giant" ?

The subject of this sketch was born in Guildhall, Vt., in the year 1792. When but a mere lad his parents moved to the White Mountains, and here he grew up a giant mountaineer, illustrating by his hardy habits, how daring enterprise and pure mountain climate nerve the man and stamp the *hero* upon mortality. Inheriting the house on the westerly end of the "Giant's Grave," with an encumbrance that made him

worse than destitute of all worldly goods, he
was one day shocked, when returning from hunt-
ing on the hills, to see his home burned down,
and his wife and infant sheltered only by an
open shed.   Twelve miles one way, and six the
other, to neighbors, here he was with his little
family in the wilderness, destitute of every comfort, save that of hope.   The sunshine of joy,
unclouded by sorrow, and the warm smiles of
good fortune seem ever attendant upon the
lives of some, constantly beckoning their favor-
ites forward to the green fields of abundance,
and bowers of pleasure and ease.   Others, perchance born under a less favoring star, in their
growth rise up like giants, breasting manfully,
step by step, the wrecking storms of adversity,
and by their own heroic exertions, hew out for
themselves characters deeply lined, amid the
black shadows of sorrow and disappointment.
Of such a mould was the spirit of Ethan A.
Crawford. The inconveniences of poverty, that
come like a strong man armed, upon poor mortality, and sickness and the many hardships
linked with everyday life in a new settlement,
fell to this man's share.   Yet he cheerfully per-
formed the duties of life with an iron resolution
that stood misfortune's shocks as firmly as his
own mountains stand storms and the changes of
time.   He was a tall, finely-proportioned man';
and, though called by many the "White Moun-

tain Giant," beneath the rough exterior of the hardy mountaineer glowed constantly in a heroic heart, the warm fire of love and manly virtue. The artless prattle of his little children was sweet music to his spirit, and his ambitious aspirations were constantly invigorated by social comfort with his little family.

The first display of Ethan's giant strength recorded is of his carrying on his head, across the Ammonoosuc river, a potash-kettle weighing four hundred pounds.

In 1821 he caught a full-grown deer, in a wild gorge, four miles from home; and as the trap had not broken his leg, and he appeared quite gentle, he thought to lead him home. Failing in his attempt to do this, he shouldered him and trudged homeward over hill and through tangled brushwood, feeling by the way, perchance, like Crusoe with his lamas, how fine it would be to have a park and many deer to show his visitors. But his day-visions vanished; for on arriving at home, he found the deer so much injured that he died.

At another time he *caught a wild mountain-buck* in a snare; and, finding him too heavy to shoulder, he made him a halter of withes, and succeeded in halter-leading him so completely, that, after nearly a day spent in the attempt, he arrived home with his prize, much to the wonder of all.

In 1829 Ethan caught a good-sized bear in a trap; and thought to bind him and lead him home as he had the buck. In attempting to do this, the bear would catch with his paws at the trees; and our hero, not willing to be outwitted by a bear, managed to get him on his shoulder, with one hand firmly hold of his nose, carried him two miles homeward. The bear, not well satisfied with his prospects, entered into a serious engagement with his captor, and by scratching and biting succeeded in tearing off his vest and one pantaloon-leg, so that Ethan laid him down so hard upon the rocks that he died. That fall he caught ten bears in that same wild glen.

The first bear kept at the White Mountains for a show was caught by Ethan, while returning from the Mountain with two young gentlemen he had been up with as guide. Seeing a small bear cross their path, they followed him to a tree which he climbed. Ethan climbed after and succeeding in getting him, tied his mouth up with a hankerchief, and backed him home. This bear he provided with a trough of water, astrap and pole; and here he was for a long time kept, as the first tame bear of the mountains. This was about the year 1829.

Ethan caught a wild cat with a birch withe, once, when passing down the Notch: he was attracted to a tree by the barking of his dog, where, up among the thick branches, he discovered a full-grown wildcat. Having only a hatchet with him, he cut two long birch withes, and twisting them well together, made a slip-noose which he run up through the thick leaves and while the cat was watching the dog, he managed to get this noose over his head, and with a sudden jerk, brought him to the ground. His dog instantly seized him, but was willing to beat a retreat till reinforced by his master, who with a heavy club came to the rescue. The skin of this cat when stretched, measured over six feet.

Ethan's two close shots are worthy of note. One fall while setting a sable line, about two miles back of the Notch, he discovered a little lake, set like a diamond in a rough frame-work of beetling crags. The fresh signs of moose near, and trout seen in its shining waters, was sufficient inducement to spend a night by its shady shore. About sunset, while engaged in catching a string of trout, his attention was suddenly arrested by a loud splashing in the still water around a rocky point, where, on looking, he saw two large brown moose pulling up lilly roots, and fighting the flies. Prepared with an extra charge, he fired, and before the first report died in echoes among the peaks, the second followed, and both moose fell dead in the lake. Ethan labored hard to drag his game ashore ; but late that evening bright visions of marrow-bones and broiled trouts flitted like realities around him. That night a doleful dirge rose in that wild gorge ; but our hero slept soundly, between two warm moose-skins. He cared not for the wild wolves that sented the taint of the fresh blood in the wind. That little mountain sheet is now, from the above circumstance, known as "Ethan's Pond."

Ethan was always proud to speak of how he carried a lady two miles down the mountain on his shoulders. It was no uncommon affair for him to shoulder a man and lug him down the mountain ; but his more delicate attempts to pack a young lady down the steep rocks, he seemed to regard as an important incident in his adventurous career. Miss E. Woodward was the name of the lady who received such marked attention from the Mountain Giant. By a wrong step she became very lame, and placeing, as well as he could, a cushion of coats upon his right shoulder, the lady became well seated, and he thus brought her down to where they left their horses.

By Adino N. Brackett's Journal, published in Moore's His. Col., vol. 1st, page 97, it appears that Adino N. Brackett, John W. Weeks, Gen. John Willson, Chas. J. Stuart, Esq., Noyes S. Dennison and Samuel A. Pearson, Esq., from Lancaster, N. H., with Philip Carrigan and E.

A. Crawford, went up July 31, 1820, to name the different summits.   *   *   *   "They made Ethan their pilot, and loaded him with provisions and blankets, like a pack-horse; and then as they began to ascend they piled on top of his load their coats." This party had a fine time and after giving the names of our sages to the different peaks according to their altitude they drank health to these hoary cliffs, in honor to the illustrions men whose names they were from this date, to bear; then curled down among the rocks without fire, on the highest crag, they doubtless spent the first night mortals ever spent on that elevated place.   In the morning after seeing the sun rise out of the ocean far, far below them, they decended westerly from the apex about a mile and came to a beautiful sheet of water (Lake of the Clouds), near a ridge of rocks which, when they left, they named "Blue Pond." It doubtless looked blue to them, for something they carried in bottles so weakened the limbs of one of the party that Ethan, was from this place burdened with a back-load of mortality, weighing two hundred pounds, down the Amonoosuc valley. Thus we find Ethan most emphatically the "Giant of the Mountains " He never hesitated to encounter. any danger that appeared in his path, whether from wild beasts, flood, or mountain tempest.

The first bridle-path on the White Moun-

tains was made in 1819.   As there had got to
be about ten or twelve visitors a year to see the
mountains, at this date, Ethan thought to accommodate his company, he would cut a path
as far as the region of scrub vegetation extended.   It had been very difficult to go without a
road, clambering over trees, up steep ledges,
through the streams and over the hedgy scrub-
growth, and accordingly when the fact of a path
being made was published, the fame of this
region spread like wild-fire.   This path was
started at the head of the notch near Gibbs'
House and extending to the top of Mount
Clinton, reached from thence to the top of Mt.
Washington, nearly where Gibbs' path now is.
Soon after the completion of this path, the ne-
cessity of a cabin where visitors could stop
through the night, was perceivable by Ethan ;
and accordingly he built a stone cabin near the
top of Mount Washington, by a spring of water
that lives there, and spread in it an abundance
soft moss for beds, that those who wished to
stop there through the night to see the sun set
and rise, might be accommodated.   This rude
home for the traveller was soon improved and
furnished with a small stove, an iron chest and
a. long roll of sheet-lead — the chest was to se-
cure from the bears and hedge-hogs the camp-
ing-blankets, and according to tradition, around
that old chest many who have hungered have

enjoyed a hearty repast. That roll of lead was for visitors to engrave their names on with a sharp iron. Alas! that tale-telling sheet has been moulded into bullets and that old chest was buried by an avalanche. How all things pass away!

In 1821 the first ladies visited Mount Washington. This party of which these ladies numbered three, had Ethan for a guide and proceeding to the stone cabin, waited there through a storm for several days, that they might be the first females to accomplish the unrecorded feat of ascending Mount Washington. This heroic little party was the Misses Austin, of Portsmouth, N. H., being accompanied by their brother and an Esq. Stuart of Lancaster. Everything was managed as much for their comfort as possible; the little cabin was provided with an outside addition, in which the gentlemen staid, that their companions might be more retired and comfortable. This party came near being what the sailors call "weather-bound." They were obliged to send back for more provisions; and at last the severe mountain-storm passed away and that for which they had ambitiously endured so much exposure was granted them. They went to the top, had a fine prospect, and, after an absence of five days, returned from the mountains, in fine spirits, highly gratified with their adventure. This heroic act should confer an honor upon the names of this pioneer party, as everything was managed with so much prudence and modesty that there was not left even a shadow for reproach, save by those who felt themselves outdone ; so says record.

In the summer of 1840 the first horse that ever climbed the rocks of Mount Washington was rode up by old Abel Crawford. The old man was then seventy-five years old, and though his head was whitened by the snows of many winters, his blood was stirred, on that occasion, by the ambitious animation of more youthful days. There he sat proudly upon his noble horse, with uncovered head, and the wind played lightly with his venerable white locks. Truly that was a picture worthy of an artist's skill. Holding that horse by the rein, there stood his son Ethan, as guide to his old father. The son and the parent!—worthy representatives of the mighty monument, to the remembrance of which, the pioneer exertions have added fadeless fame. From that day a new era dawned on these mountains. Forget not the veteran Abel, and Ethan *"the White Mountain Giant."*

By record it appears that this remarkable defile was known to the aborigines, but it was never used by them as a crossing-place for their captives, or as a war-path, till white explorers in part wiped from their moral vision the dark superstition that such approach to Agiochook would be deemed by the Great Spirit pardonless sacrilege. For many years after it was known to the first hunters this Notch became forgotten or neglected, till the year 1771, when it was re-discovered by two hunters, *Nash* and *Sawyer*. They drove a moose up a wild mountain stream, surrounded by towering crags ; and, with a be-lief that it was a deep gorge, surrounded behind by mountains, they followed, animated by the thought of making an easy conquest of their intended victim. Imagine their disappointment when they found their purpose thwarted by tracing the foot-prints of the moose along an ancient Indian trail, over high precipices, to a little meadow quite on the other side of the mountain ! These hunters published this inter-esting discovery, and were rewarded by the tract of land, northerly from the Notch, known as "Nash and Sawyer's Location."

The first settler through the Notch was Col. Whipple, from Portsmouth, N. H. He came up in the year 1772, and he was at the time enabled to get his cattle up through the Notch by the means of teacles and ropes, as the hunter's path was over several precipices, now shunned by the travelled way. All the way through the northern wilderness of Laconia (now N. H.), with the needful means of civili-zation with him, he came, scaled the crags that hang around that mighty rent through mountains, and by his enterprise earned the honor of being the first white man who made a permanent settlement in the township of Dartmouth (now Jefferson.)

The first female through the Notch was one who in her old age was known as "Granny Stalbird." She came up with Col. Whipple in 1776, as his servant-girl. Afterwards she married, became a widow ; since which, learning of the Indians the virtue of roots and herbs, she became a noted doctress, and was famous in all this new country for her skill. After enjoying life for nearly a full century, she died, leaving her name in the memory of many pleasantly cherished ; and the history of a vast rock, that long ago tumbled down from the mountains, bears the name "Granny Stalbird's Rock." One time, while passing on her professional duties through the Notch, she was overtaken by a terrible storm ; and darkness coming on, with torrents of water from the clouds, that swelled to a fearful height the wild mountain streams, she sought shelter under this rock, and laid there through a sleepless night, with the doleful music of water, wind and wolves about her. The habits of this useful old doctress were quite masculine. On foot or astride of an old horse, she might commonly be seen in the road, hastening from house to house on her errands of mercy. Bad travelling and severe storms, were never insurmountable barriers in her path of usefulness. To do good to the sick was her life; and her God sustained her for long years as a worthy ministering spirit to the afflicted. She needs no monument to her memory more lasting than that which lives in her deeds.

The Willey House is the oldest building erected in the Notch. This was built in the year 1793, by a Mr. Davis, to accommodate the unfortunate 'storm-bound traveller, who, from curiosity, or on business, might dare the dangers of this will pass. Then a little grassy meadow stretched along the bank of the Saco; tall rock-maples, and a towering mountain barrier, rose in the background from this little home of the pilgrim. How like a cool shadow of a great rock was this retreat among the frowning crags! But the thundering avalanche came, and, since August 28th, 1826, the spirit of desolation has brooded over that fated spot. How lonely there is the dirge of the high wind, as it sweeps down that solitary chasm; and the wail of the sunset breeze, with the loud requiem of the on-rushing hurricane, is most mournful, for human bones are there palled in an avalanche's ruins!

www.ingramcontent.com/pod-product-compliance
Lightning Source LLC
Chambersburg PA
CBHW061240260626
47172CB00003B/938